WONDER BOOKS®

Sharing

A Level Three Reader

By Kathryn Kyle

On the cover...
Two sisters share an umbrella on a rainy day.

Published by The Child's World®, Inc.
PO Box 326
Chanhassen, MN 55317-0326
800-599-READ
www.childsworld.com

Special thanks to the Campe family and Shoesmith Elementary School
for their help and cooperation in preparing this book.

Photo Credits
© Bettmann/CORBIS: 25
© David Young-Wolff/PhotoEdit: cover
© Gavin Wickham, Eye Ubiquitous/CORBIS: 22
© John Terence Turner/FPG International: 17
© Kelly/Mooney Photography/CORBIS: 13
© Mark E. Gibson/Unicorn Stock Photos: 6
© Michael Newman/PhotoEdit: 26
© Myrleen Ferguson Cate/PhotoEdit: 21
© Romie Flanagan: 3, 5, 10, 18
© Steve Bourgeois/Unicorn Stock Photos: 14
© Tom McCarthy/Unicorn Stock Photos: 9

Project Coordination: Editorial Directions, Inc.
Photo Research: Alice K. Flanagan

Library of Congress Cataloging-in-Publication Data
Kyle, Kathryn.
Sharing / by Kathryn Kyle.
p. cm. — (Wonder books)
Includes index.
Summary: Provides everyday examples of what it means to share.
ISBN 1-56766-093-2 (library bound : alk. paper)
1. Sharing—Juvenile literature. [1. Sharing.]
I. Title. II. Wonder books (Chanhassen, Minn.)
BJ1533.G4 .K95 2002
177'.7—dc21
2001007947

What is sharing? Sharing is working with other people and giving them something you have. Sharing is an important part of getting along with others.

A friend might not have any markers for drawing. You have a new set of markers. Sharing is letting your friend use your new markers.

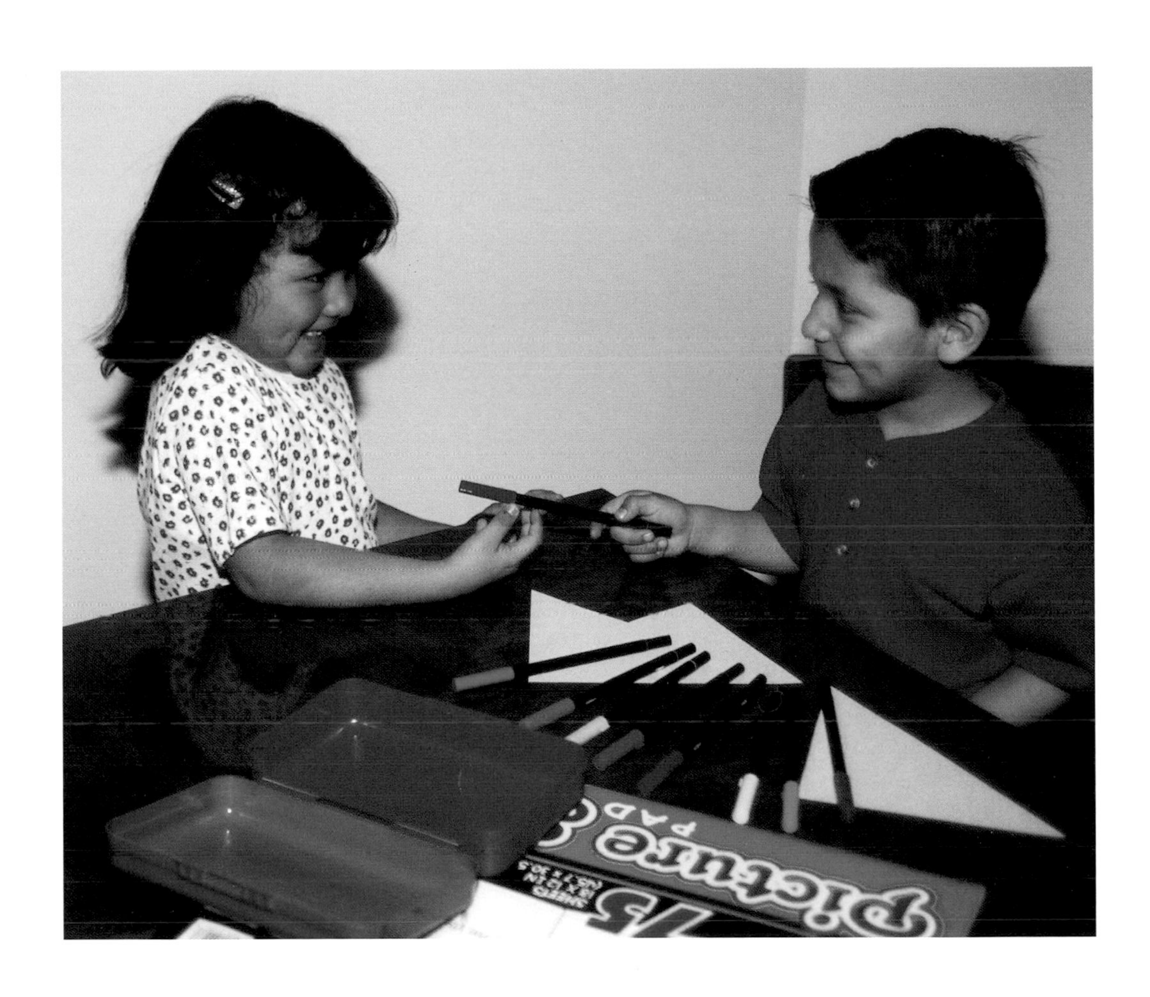
Picture
PAD

At a Fourth of July picnic, there is one big slice of watermelon. Everyone wants to have some. Sharing is letting your friends eat the watermelon with you.

A friend wants to play baseball. He does not have a ball. Sharing is bringing your ball to the park so you can play together.

On the bus, you have a seat all to yourself. The bus is very crowded. There are no more empty seats. One more person gets on the bus. Sharing is letting that person sit with you.

You make a wonderful picture on the computer. It is one of the best pictures you have ever done. Sharing is showing the picture to your grandfather. He is so happy to see one of your pictures.

Friends share many things. Sometimes your friend might be sad. Your friend needs someone to listen to. Sharing is taking time to listen to your friend.

Sometimes your friend might be very happy. Your friend wants to share good news with you. Sharing is listening to your friend and being happy for her.

Many things happen all day at school. Your family is interested in what you do at school. Sharing is telling them about your day.

Sharing also means showing others how you feel about them. One way to share your love is to share a smile. Another way is to give someone a hug. That's the best kind of sharing!

Many people in history have shared with others in important ways. One of these people was Mother Teresa. She was a **Catholic nun** who lived in India. She studied to be a teacher. Mother Teresa lived among the needy and helped make their lives better.

← This is a picture of Mother Teresa.

In 1979, Mother Teresa won the **Nobel Peace Prize** for her work. She shared her love and life with poor people around the world. She was a wonderful example of someone who shared her life with others. Mother Teresa died in 1997.

This picture shows Mother Teresa holding a young boy in India.

Sharing is important. It makes others feel good. It makes you feel good, too. What have you shared today?

At Home

- Share your favorite toy with a friend.
- Let your brother or sister play with your birthday presents.
- Tell your parents that you love them.

At School

- Share your snack with a classmate who doesn't have one.
- Share responsibility for cleaning up the classroom with your teacher.
- Let a friend use your jump rope on the playground.

In Your Community

- Ask an adult to help you give your outgrown clothes and toys to the needy.
- Bake cookies to give to a bake sale.
- Give part of your babysitting money to a homeless shelter.

Glossary

Catholic (KATH-uh-lik)
The Catholic Church is a Christian church that has the pope as its leader.

Nobel Peace Prize (No-BELL PEESS PRIZE)
The Nobel Peace Prize is an award given to people who work to bring about peace. Mother Teresa won the award in 1979.

nun (NUN)
A nun is a woman who dedicates her life to God, the church, and caring for others.

Index

baseball, 8
bus, 11
computer, 12
Fourth of July, 7
grandfather, 12
history, 23
hug, 20
India, 23
markers, 4
Mother Teresa, 23, 24
Nobel Peace Prize, 24
smile, 20
watermelon, 7

To Find Out More

Books

Barraclough, John. *Mother Teresa.* Chicago, Ill.: Heinemann Library, 1997.

Bridwell, Norman. *The Cat and the Bird in the Hat.* New York: Scholastic, 2000.

Pienkowski, Jan. *Bel and Bub and the Big Brown Box.* New York: Dorling Kindersley, 2000.

Riley, Susan. *Sharing.* Chanhassen, Minn.: Child's World, 2000.

Weinberger, Kimberly. *Share-and-Be-Fair Sticker Book.* New York: Cartwheel Books, 2001.

Web Sites

Children's Stories
http://www.wildgear.com/stories/corbett.html
To read a short story about sharing.

National 4-H Council
http://www.areyouintoit.com/
To find out about ways kids can volunteer in their communities.

Note to Parents and Educators

Welcome to Wonder Books®! These books provide text at three different levels for beginning readers to practice and strengthen their reading skills. Additionally, the use of nonfiction text provides readers the valuable opportunity to *read to learn*, not just to learn to read.

These leveled readers allow children to choose books at their level of reading confidence and performance. Nonfiction Level One books offer beginning readers simple language, word choice, and sentence structure as well as a word list. Nonfiction Level Two books feature slightly more difficult vocabulary, longer sentences, and longer total text. In the back of each Nonfiction Level Two book are an index and a list of books and Web sites for finding out more information. Nonfiction Level Three books continue to extend word choice and length of text. In the back of each Nonfiction Level Three book are a glossary, an index, and a list of books and Web sites for further research.

State and national standards in reading and language arts emphasize using nonfiction at all levels of reading development. Wonder Books® fill the historical void in nonfiction material for primary grade readers with the additional benefit of a leveled text.

About the Author

Kathryn Kyle has taught elementary school and writes extensively for children. She lives in Minnesota.